All children have
a great ambition to read
to themselves . . .

and a sense of achievement when they can do so.
The **read it yourself** *series has been devised to*
satisfy their ambition. Since many children learn
from the Ladybird Key Words Reading Scheme,
these stories have been based to a large extent
on the Key Words List, and the tales chosen are
those with which children are likely to be familiar.

The series can of course be used as
supplementary reading for any reading scheme.
Red Riding Hood is intended for children
reading up to Book 3c of the Ladybird Reading
Scheme. The following words are additional to
the vocabulary used at that level –

Riding, Hood, Grandma, goodbye, bad,
wolf, does, runs, cupboard, hat, shawl,
eyes, ears, hear, teeth, eat, she, her,
big, not

A list of other titles at the same level will be
found on the back cover.

Published by Ladybird Books Ltd Loughborough Leicestershire UK
Ladybird Books Inc Lewiston Maine 04240 USA
© LADYBIRD BOOKS LTD MCMLXXVII

Red Riding Hood

by Fran Hunia
illustrated by Kathie Layfield

Ladybird Books

This is Red Riding Hood.

She is at home

playing with her toys.

Red Riding Hood's Mummy

says, Come here,

Red Riding Hood.

Grandma is at home in bed.

I have some cakes for her.

I want you to go

and give the cakes

to Grandma, please.

Yes, says Red Riding Hood.

I want to go

and see Grandma.

I can give her the cakes.

Mummy gives the cakes
to Red Riding Hood.

Goodbye,
says Red Riding Hood.

Goodbye,
says her Mummy.
See that the big bad wolf
does not get you.

Red Riding Hood sees
some trees
and some flowers.

Grandma likes flowers,
she says.
I can get some flowers
for Grandma.

The big bad wolf
sees Red Riding Hood.

Come and play with me,
he says.

No, says Red Riding Hood.
I can not play with you.
I have to go
and see Grandma.
She is in bed.
I have some cakes
and flowers for her.

The wolf runs
to Grandma's home.

He says, Grandma, Grandm

I want to come in.

Grandma is in bed.

Is that you,

Red Riding Hood?

she says.

Yes, says the big bad wolf.

Grandma gets up.

She sees the wolf.

Help, help, she says.

She gets up into a cupboar

The big bad wolf comes in.

He gets Grandma's hat
and shawl, and jumps
into Grandma's bed.

Red Riding Hood

has the cakes

and the flowers.

She comes

to Grandma's home.

Grandma, she says,

it is Red Riding Hood.

Please can I come in?

Yes, says the big bad wolf.

You can come in.

I want to see you,

Red Riding Hood.

Red Riding Hood comes in.

She says, Look, Grandma.

I have some cakes
and some flowers for you.

She looks at the wolf.

He is in Grandma's bed.

He has Grandma's hat
and shawl on.

You have big eyes,

Grandma,

says Red Riding Hood.

Yes, says the wolf.

They are good

to see you with.

You have big ears,

Grandma,

says Red Riding Hood.

Yes, says the wolf.

They are good

to hear you with.

You have big teeth,

Grandma,

says Red Riding Hood.

Yes, says the big bad wolf.

They are good

to eat you with.

The wolf jumps up.

Help, help,

says Red Riding Hood.

She runs and runs.

Red Riding Hood sees
a man.

It is her Daddy.

Help, help, she says.

Here comes a wolf.

He is a big one.

He wants to eat me up.

Get up into a tree,

Red Riding Hood,

says her Daddy.

I can get

that big bad wolf.

Red Riding Hood gets
up in a tree.

Her Daddy gets the wolf.

Red Riding Hood
comes down.

She says, Please come
and help me
to look for Grandma.

They go to Grandma's home

Grandma is in the cupboard

Help, help, she says.

I want to get down.

Red Riding Hood
and her Daddy
get Grandma down.

They help her into bed.

I have some cakes
and flowers for you,
says Red Riding Hood.

She gives the cakes
and flowers to Grandma.

You are a good girl,
says Grandma.
The cakes look good.
We can have cakes for tea.

You have the cakes,

Grandma,

says Red Riding Hood.

We have to go home for tea

Come on, Daddy.

It was good to see you,

says Grandma.

Here is an apple for you

and one for Daddy.

Goodbye, Red Riding Hood.

Goodbye.